Wishful Thinking

Check out the other books in the

series:

The Cursed Coin

Picture Day

Framed for Life

#GraveyardChallenge

FRIGHTVISION

Wishful Thinking

John Zakour

Culliver Crantz

J
ZAKOUR
JOHN

Cover Design: Stephanie Gaston

www.FrightVisionBooks.com

Facebook: @FrightVisionBooks

Dearest Visitor,

Welcome!

I hope you enjoy your time with us. Be careful letting your mind wander ... You never know what it might wish for.

Pay attention if you dare, but only if you're not too scared.

Your nightmare is ready. Let's begin!

Sweetest Dreams,

Crantz

CHAPTER ONE
TAMMY

It was a beautiful fall day. My twin brother Barry and I were walking to the Spring City Used Antique shop. Our mom's birthday was coming up and we wanted to get her something. The problem was, we were on a limited budget. A very limited budget. Hence the reason we were forced to shop at the Used Antique Shop.

"How much do we have to spend?" Barry asked me.

Reaching into my pocket, I pulled out the sad amount of money Barry and I had managed to save this year for mom's birthday. Two fives, three ones, and some cents. "Thirteen dollars!" I told Barry.

Barry smiled and shrugged. "Hey, it's not as much as I hoped but it's something!"

"I wish we could have done better," I sighed.

1

"Yeah if wishes were fishes, we'd all swim in riches," Barry answered.

"Do you have any idea what that means?" I asked my bro.

He shrugged. "No idea. Grandma Mimaw always says that. I love her, so I take her word for it."

"I love her too, but she is a weird one!" I said.

"Yeah that makes her more loveable!" Barry smiled.

As we walked towards the store, I couldn't help thinking how disappointed I was with us. Every year since we were ten, Barry and I swore we would save up our money and buy Mom a nice gift for her birthday. After all it's been just Mom and us and our dog Rover for a long time now. Mom is such an amazing woman. She teaches and does research all day at Spring City University, yet still, is always there for us. She takes me to soccer practice and Barry to band and his debate club. She takes us both to karate. My gosh, she does our stinky laundry twice a week and never complains. Yet all we can do is raise a lousy 13 dollars!

"We kind of suck," I told Barry.

Barry stopped and looked at me with his eyes wide open. "Wait? What? We do? Why?" He stopped walking and scratched his head. "Why?" he repeated. "Thirteen dollars is our best haul ever!"

2

Barry was always a bright side kind of kid. He saw the best in people and in any situation. I kind of envied him. I think life is easier when you are simple. Okay that might be a bit harsh. After all, Barry always got good grades and he was on the debate team. However, he took easier classes and to my knowledge, he never won a debate. Barry always said he loved to talk and talk loud. Debate let him do both. I never told him that louder doesn't mean better or right.

Shaking my head, I sighed. "We're 13 now. Surely we can come up with more than 13 dollars."

Barry smiled. "Hey, don't call me Shirley!" he joked. Oh yeah, Barry also considered himself to be a first-class pun master. He was more like a third or fourth-class pun dunce.

Barry gave me a friendly little push. "Admit that's punny!" he said, smiling. "Man, these puns just come naturally to me. I'm pretty sure it's only a matter of time before I write the next Calvin and Hobbs comic. Yep, I'm that good."

I had to give Barry some props. He wasn't lacking in confidence.

"Now if you sold some of your puns to make some money, then I might admit that you have some potential," I said.

"You mean pun-tential right?" He said, nudging me with his elbow.

Argh. He was killing me. And now, I started to wish we had taken a different route to the Used Antique shop. For some strange reason, the town had built their newest building—a glowing bright, twenty four-hour convenience store called 24-7 next to the antique store. It made for a great contrast, I guess. But the 24-7 had become the hangout for the "cool kids" in our Spring City Middle School. Barry and I were eighth graders, but we certainly weren't the "cool ones," and yes, I used air quotes when I said it.

Of course, standing outside of the 24-7 sipping on a cold drink and looking at their phones were Mo and Maggie Brown. Mo was a big dude, maybe the biggest eighth graders in town, if not the state. He had long hair that he never combed, yet he never seemed to care. Maggie was short with blonde hair and green eyes that she would use to look down on almost anybody. She scared me way more than Mo. Maggie and Mo were always backed up by Ned and Fred Rock. The Rocks and the Browns were literally the scourge of my existence.

I bent down, trying to make myself look smaller and invisible as we walked by. I hoped they wouldn't notice me. I wished they wouldn't notice me. *Just walk by nice and quiet and all will be well*, I thought. They were so busy snap-chatting to themselves, I hoped that they wouldn't look up and see Barry and me walking by.

I held my breath, somehow thinking it would make me walk more silently. It appeared to be working. We got past them without anyone noticing. Just a few more yards and we would be safely in the Used Antique store.

Barry suddenly noticed the four 'cool kids.' "Hey guys!" he yelled out, waving to them while jumping up and down to make sure he got their attention.

Maggie spotted us first. She stuffed her phone in her pocket and walked towards us. Mo, Ned and Fred followed like geese.

"Man, I wish you hadn't done that!" I whispered to Barry.

"Oh, they only tease us because they like us." He smiled.

"I wish they liked us a little less then."

Maggie reached us. "Hey, losers! I'm surprised your mommy lets you walk downtown all by yourselves."

Barry nodded and grinned. "Yeah, we've been doing that for a while now!"

The guys behind Maggie laughed, then she did, too.

"My god, you two are such winners!" she said.

"Thanks!" Barry said, not noticing her sarcasm. Even though he was on the debate team, he didn't pick up on clues very well.

The four kids laughed.

Maggie locked her mean green eyes on me. "I looked at the soccer schedule. My team plays your team this week. Ha! We are undefeated! How many games has your team won?"

I felt quite certain she already knew the answer.

"Ah, one," I said holding up my pointer finger. I didn't tell her that our only win was a forfeit because the other team had food poisoning. A win is a win.

"We're going to crush you guys!" Maggie said, looking down at my legs. "I'd wear extra shin guards if I were you!" Her voice was calm, yet threatening.

They all laughed and walked away.

"Told you they liked us!" Barry said.

"Man, I wish I could shut that girl up for good!" I said.

Barry put his arm around me and led me into the store. "Sis, you need to look for the good in people!"

"I'd need a super electron microscope to find the good in Maggie!"

"Now, you're just making words up!"

We walked into the Used Antique Shop. The place smelled old and dusty, even though it looked really clean. A tall, blonde, older woman at the counter looked up at us and smiled. "Hello, Barry and Tammy!" she said.

Was I hearing things? "How do you know our names?"

The woman's eyes opened wide. "I am a gypsy queen. I know all and tell some!" she said with a wry smile.

"Cool!" Barry pumped his fist.

"No, really?" What kind of response was that? I needed to know what the deal was, otherwise I was ready to leave.

"I went to grad school with your mother Linda," the lady said. "Tell her Kate says hi."

"Kate who?" I asked, trying to get her last name.

"Just Kate," she said. "What can I help you two with? If I remember correctly, your mom has a birthday coming up."

"She does!" Barry said, not nearly as freaked out by her remembering that as I was. "Man, you have a great memory!"

Kate smiled and pointed at her head. "Comes from being a gypsy queen! You kids look around and call me if you have any questions."

"Alright! Thanks!" Barry said.

We walked up and down the aisles of the old store. One only had furniture made of old wood and wicker, mostly chairs and little side tables.

"What about this chair?" Barry pointed at a creaking old chair.

"Why would mom want that?" I asked.

"To sit in after a long day," Barry said.

"We have a lot of chairs already!"

He sat down, ignoring my differing opinion. He wiggled his butt. "This chair is fun! It moves!"

"I don't think it's supposed to do that. Stop! You're gonna break the chair!" I reached down and pulled him back to his feet.

Barry wasn't happy about my aggressive actions, but the chair was way more than $13, so we couldn't afford to have him do something stupid and break it. Otherwise, we'd be broke and have no present for Mom.

I got him away from the chairs and we walked down a different aisle; this one had candles, old lights, and jewelry of all colors and shapes. Barry grabbed a nice jade necklace. "This is pretty!" he said.

I looked at it. "Yeah of course, and do you see how much it costs? $100!"

"Oh, that's a tad out of our price range!" Barry gently put the necklace down.

"Yeah, I wish we could afford that, but we can't."

Kate walked over to us. "I see you kids are having trouble finding something just right for your mom."

I nodded. "Yeah, sadly we don't have a lot to spend," I sighed. "I wish we did."

She pointed to shelves filled with all sorts of small objects. "Why not try the keepsakes and knickknacks aisle?" she suggested.

We walked down that aisle, which was full of old paintings, wood toys, stuffed animals, old silverware, a couple of hats, and a few decks of cards. Everything looked either too expensive or too crappy.

Kate must have sensed my frustration. She stopped stocking the shelves nearby us and asked, "How much do you kids have to spend?"

Before I could say ten dollars, hoping that she would give us a deal, Barry blurted, "Thirteen dollars!" way more proudly than he should have.

Kate tapped her cheek and smiled. She reached up to the top shelf and pulled down an old glass test tube. It appeared to be empty, yet it still had a cork sealing it.

"I know your mom, she'll get a kick out of this. This is one of the test tubes we used in college."

"I don't know," I said.

"I'll give it to you for free!" Kate said.

"Sold!" I said, taking it from her hand.

Kate smiled. "It's an antique, your mom will love it." She tapped the top. "But whatever you do, don't pull out the cork." She looked serious and I thought she was joking at first. I even giggled a little, but her face remained like stone.

"Ah, why not?" Barry asked. "Does it have stink gas in it?"

Kate thought for a second before she nodded. "Yeah, that's it. Trust me, what's in there really stinks! Just leave it be. Your mom will be happy. Everybody will be happy!"

That was weird, but we had our present. She gave us a small bag and we left thinking that Kate may not have answered our wishes, but she made our lives easier.

As we walked out the door, we heard her call to us, "Remember—whatever you do, do NOT open that test tube!"

CHAPTER TWO
BARRY

That test tube was so cool! I actually thought about keeping it for myself. We could go try and find Mom something else, maybe pick her some flowers. "Let's hide it my room!" I said, even though I didn't really have a good reason for doing that. I just wanted to be the one who held Mom's gift until we gave it to her, or keep it.

"Your room stinks!" Tammy argued. "It should go in my room."

Man, fart a few times in your own room and leave dirty socks around and your sister marks you for life. It's not like Tammy's farts smelled like roses. But, I figured I could use the stink to my advantage. Lifting my pointer finger I said, "All the more reason why we should keep the test tube in my room. Mom won't hang around there very long."

11

"Nobody can or they would pass out," Tammy countered. "But you have a point. That is a safe spot."

We walked up the stairs to my bedroom. Tammy stopped outside the door. "Open your window before I go in there."

I walked into my room, shaking my head. It really didn't smell that bad in here. Well, I looked at my desk and noticed that my cactus plant had died. That had to be a coincidence. I opened my window and waved some fresh air into the room.

After taking a deep breath, I decided it smelled okay. "You can come in now!"

Tammy walked in slowly as she sniffed the air. "It's still fairly nasty!" she said. "But it might make sense to hide Mom's present in here." Tammy pulled the test tube out of her pocket. She held it up to her eyes and walked over to the window. She leaned her head out of the window and breathed in some fresh air. She popped her head back into the room. She looked again at the tube.

"That is so weird," Tammy said.

"What?" I looked at the tube. "I don't see anything but a cool empty test tube."

"Exactly!" Tammy said, looking at it with one eye shut. She shook it. Holding it up to the light, she looked at it again. "It seems very, very empty—"

"Can something really be very, very empty?" I asked, feeling like I was in the midst of a debate team match.

"You make another good point," she said while tapping the cork. "But why seal an empty test tube?" she asked.

"Why not seal it?" I asked, imagining the debate team teacher praising my question.

Tammy rolled her eyes. "Now I see why you never win your debates."

"That was a winning point. And I finished second in that one debate!" I said. "Out of three people!"

"Yeah, second is not winning."

Didn't matter. I loved debating with people. To me it was fun and exciting. Debating got my heart pumping. But of course, I knew there was no debating with my stubborn sister. "Okay, what's your point?" I asked her.

Tammy showed me the test tube. "Well, a closed test tube won't do Mom much good. There's not much you can do with a tube you can't put anything in."

"You can look at it ... and it looks cool!" I told my sister. For some reason, I didn't want to open the test tube. It felt wrong, especially after that nice lady, Kate, from the store told us not to. She had said that whatever was in there really stunk and I believed her, but I wasn't sure why.

Tammy rolled her eyes. "Yeah, but if we open it, Mom can put a flower or two in it. Imagine this as a vase. Then it would look even cooler and it'd be functional."

I looked at it. Tammy had a point. I guess my sis was pretty smart. But still this nagged at me. "Why would Kate have told us not to open the test tube? There might be something bad in it!"

"Why would she give us a test tube that *actually* had something bad in it?" Tammy asked.

I nodded in agreement. "Maybe you should be on the debate team."

Tammy took out her phone and typed something. "I'm looking up the Used Antique's Shop's web site. Maybe I can learn more about Kate." A pause and a bit more typing. "Yep, she was in Mom's class at Cornell University. She got her Master's in Psychology. She worked for years as a psychologist helping senior citizens and she's also a dog trainer."

As if on cue, our Border Collie, Rover, walked into my room. "Woof!" Rover barked, wagging his tail. I bent down to pet him. "Hey boy, did you have a nice nap?" I asked.

"Woof!" he repeated.

"Pretty sure that means yes!" I told Tammy. "I do speak fluent dog."

"I think it means your room doesn't stink as much as normal, so he feels it's safe to come in now," Tammy countered. "If he could talk he'd tell you that!"

"Ha!" I said.

Tammy held her heart. "Ouch, witty retort!" She bent down and petted Rover. "Poor boy having to put up with the smell in here with your sensitive nose!"

Tammy held up the test tube again. "I say we open it!"

Once my sister got a thought in her head, there really was no stopping her. No logic could hold her back. She became a girl on a mission.

"How can we be sure there's no poison gas in there?" I asked.

Tammy rolled her eyes at me again. "You don't put poison gas in a test tube and leave it at an antique store." She walked towards the window. "But if it makes you feel better, I'll lean out of the window and open it. Without a bit of hesitation, Tammy grabbed hold of the cork. She tugged on it, trying to pry it out of the tube. It was stuck. She grunted and growled. It looked like she was going to squeeze the tube too tight and it would smash to pieces. She grunted one last time and the cork popped out. Our eyes opened wide when a mist floated out of the tube.

I dove to the ground, covering my face. "O-M-G! Open the window!" I shouted. "You're going to kill us all!"

15

Tammy actually listened to me and pushed the window up hard. A look of panic crossed her face as she turned her back to the window and breathed a little sigh of relief. "Wow that was so close!" she said. "I can't believe you were actually right about something!"

Slowly, I picked up my head. I couldn't see the smoke in the room anymore. I was still alive. There wasn't anything to worry about. I thought, anyway.

Knock! Knock! Something was at the window.

CHAPTER THREE
STILL BARRY

I was afraid to look. But, after the second knock, I peered outside. There, floating and waving, was a tall, slim, woman with jet black hair and bright blue eyes. She wore a long, flowing, red dress. She was waving at us.

"Okay, now this is different," Tammy said.

The woman didn't wait for us to open the window. She slid underneath the crack at the bottom of the window and stood in my room. She stared at us and said, "Finally, I'm out of that tube!" She arched her back, stretching out. "Kind of cramped in there." She sniffed the air. "Why does it smell like dead sheep in here?" She snapped her fingers and suddenly, my room smelled like fresh roses. The woman smiled. "Ah, much better."

"Agreed," Tammy said. "Who the heck are you?"

"Oh wow!" I gasped.

The woman bowed. "I'm Genny the genie. I can grant you every wish!"

"Really?" Tammy asked.

Genny smiled and winked. "Try me, honey!"

"I wish Rover could talk!" Tammy blurted.

Genny snapped her fingers. "Done."

Rover coughed to clear his throat then looked at me. "Dude, I love ya but your sister's right. Your room did stink before Genny's magic cleaned it." Rover smiled. "Luckily I don't mind a good stink."

"Wow you can talk!!" I shouted. "This is great! Now we can truly be best buds."

Rover grinned at me, "I'm your best bud whether I can talk or not."

Tammy didn't seem to pay much attention to Rover as she was far more interested in Genny. She asked, "So how many wishes do we get?"

Genny smiled. "Unlimited! Just as long as you sign the contract and don't reseal me in the tube." Genny snapped her fingers and a tablet appeared in her hand. On the screen was microscopic text.

Tammy leaned in and tried to read it. She flicked through the lines with her finger. "Where do I sign?" she asked.

"Just click agree at the bottom," Genny said with a mischievous smile.

"Do you humans ever read those things?" Rover asked.

Tammy's finger hung in the air, ready to click. "They're all the same," she shrugged. "I mean, come on, who wouldn't want unlimited wishes?"

"Have you ever heard the saying too much of a good thing?" Rover asked. "How do you know this genie lady isn't evil?"

"I have a good feeling about her!" Tammy said.

"But I don't!" Rover said, sniffing closer to Genny. "Her scent is off!"

Tammy rolled her eyes at Rover. "You drink from the toilet. And well, you're a dog!"

Rover nodded. "True, but I'm a smart dog. I listen to things."

"Don't worry, doggie," Genny said in a slow, soothing voice. "Wishes drain me a little, so I will make sure the kids are careful." Genny showed me the tablet. "For this to be binding, I need both of you to agree."

"I have a question," I said.

"I'm sure I have the answer," Genny said.

"Did that old Kate lady know you were in this test tube?"

"I'm not in that cramped tube any longer!" Genny said, tipping the tube upside down. "Nothing is!"

"Did she know?" I asked.

Genny laughed. "No, of course not. If she did, don't you think she would have used the wishes for herself? I mean everybody loves having wishes. Right?"

I thought about what she said. It did make sense. I reached for the tablet. I stopped. "Wait."

"Oh, come on!" Tammy said, stomping her feet. She must've had some wishes ready because she was acting very impatient.

"What if we want to undo a wish?" I asked, ignoring her tantrum.

Tammy actually stopped and listened. "That is a very good question."

Genny patted me on the head. I kind of liked it. "You are a smart young lad for asking. Once a wish is made you can't undo it. It's one of the rules."

Genny quickly scrolled to Section 4 Line 13: *Once made, a wish cannot be unmade.*

"I'm not sure I like that," I thought out loud.

Genny laughed. "You are two really smart kids. I'm sure you will use your wishes wisely."

Rover looked at us both. "I love you two, but I'm not sure about this."

Genny crossed her arms and tapped her foot. "The dog who has been able to talk for five minutes may be right. You two might not be smart enough to handle me. Maybe I should find someone else who wants *unlimited* wishes. Think that'll be tough?"

"Wait we're smart enough!" Tammy insisted.

"Yeah we are!" I agreed.

"Why were you in the bottle in the first place?" Rover asked. He shot Tammy and I each a look. "You know it's bad when your dog is the voice of reason."

Genny grinned. "My last owner was some guy named Gates."

"Bill Gates?" I asked.

Genny smiled and pointed at me. "Yeah, that nerdy guy. I made him super, duper, uber rich. Once he had everything he wanted, he gave me away. Besides, taking a geek who didn't even graduate from college and making him one of the richest men in the world did take a LOT of magic. I needed time in my tube to recharge my power!" Genny flexed her muscles. "Now I'm charged and ready to grant wishes again!" She showed us the tablet again. "All you need to do is sign your agreement, "then I will make you very happy by granting your every wish!"

Tammy looked at me. "What could go wrong?"

"A lot of things! So many things!" Rover said.

Tammy leaned in and clicked the agree button. The tablet made a beeping sound. Tammy turned to me and smiled. She was the smartest person I knew besides Mom. That's right, Mom. "Maybe we should run this by Mom?" I asked.

"Your mom will think you're crazy. Only you two can see me. And if you tell anybody else about me, your wishes stop!" Genny answered.

"Now that seems a bit convenient!" Rover said.

"It sure does!" I said. But, I trusted my sister. I leaned in and touched the agree button. The tablet made a series of nice beeping sounds. Balloons fell down from the ceiling on us.

"You made the right choice!" Genny exclaimed. "Trust me when I say you can trust me!"

CHAPTER FOUR
TAMMY

O-M-G this was amazing! Amaze-balls! We had our own genie with unlimited wishes. This was going to be so much fun! I started rubbing my hands together in excitement. I looked at Genny. "Okay, let's start with something basic and easy!"

"Whatever you wish is yours," Genny said with a bow.

"I want cookies. Lots of cookies!" I said. "More cookies than I know what to do with."

My bro rubbed his stomach and added, "I want pies: apple, pecan, pumpkin, cherry, berry, and chocolate!"

Genny folded her arms. "You guys don't think very big. Do you?"

"This is just a warm up," I told her. "Your test."

Barry's room filled with all sorts of cookies and pies. Wherever there had been empty space, there was now either a stack of cookies or a sweet-smelling pie.

"Wish granted!" Genny said.

Rover looked around. "Oh my! Am I the only one who thinks this is a bad idea? Are you kids really just going to eat these without …," Rover was too late, we had already begun devouring the food. "Guess so," he said.

"Yes!" I cheered, diving into the cookies and stuffing my mouth with them. The cookies were sweet, better than anything I had ever tasted. It felt like I was eating pure deliciousness. But, while the cookies were tasty this was only the start. We had a genie! Imagine all of the things I would be able to do! I had to admit that there were a lot of people I wanted to get even with. Okay, maybe not a lot, but certainly a few.

Looking over at Barry, I stopped to watch as he gobbled the pies right down to the bottom of their plates.

"This is by far the best pie I've ever tasted!" Barry mumbled with pie crumbs covering his face. He dove into another gooey cherry pie.

"Agreed, these cookies rock!" I said, woofing big chocolate chip cookies down as fast as I could grab them. All the while, I was thinking of ways I could get revenge on people who ticked me off.

Rover didn't help us eat anything. He just shook his head and lectured. "You're eating too fast! You're eating too much! You kids are like animals! And not in a good way!"

We both ignored Rover. After all, he was our pet. We weren't about to take advice from a dog who liked to sniff other dog's butts. I kept eating, and so did Barry.

Suddenly, I felt my stomach rumble. Actually, I felt it quake. Yes, I felt like I had a 7.0 earthquake going on in my gut. I stood up, placing my hand over my stomach. "Oh no, I don't feel so hot."

Barry looked at me. "You look a little blueish green."

Looking at him, he too looked blueish green, and his eyes were puffy. "You don't look much better," I said, barely able to talk.

I felt like a billion cookies were pushing to leave my body and as quickly as possible. My stomach churned. Holding my hand over my mouth I raced to Barry's bathroom. Out of the corner of my eye, I saw Barry holding his stomach and heading in the same direction. I needed to beat him there. We both needed to barf and I wanted my barf to hit the toilet first. Not sure why, I guess I figured that way he'd be smelling my barf, not the other way around.

Flying to the toilet, I dropped to my knees and literally let it all out. I won't go into the gory details, but it was a mix of green, blue, and grey slime.

"Oh sis, please move over," Barry begged. "I don't want to puke on your back!"

Glancing up from the toilet I ordered, "You better not!" Then I turned my head and threw up some more. After a deep breath I looked up.

Barry pleaded at me with his eyes. "I don't want to," he said gagging on the words. "But soon this will be out of my control."

I moved farther over to the side of the toilet. I felt pretty certain that nothing else could come out of me. I had already released my weight in barf.

Barry dropped to the spot I had been. Barf instantly flooded out of his mouth. Me going first didn't make it any better. In fact, the combination of both of our puke smelled even worse than I thought would be possible. Think onions and sardines mixed with socks, wet dogs, and rotten cheese. Take that stink and triple it. I stood up and looked away. I still couldn't block out the sound of Barry gagging and belching.

"Oh bro, so not cool," I said.

Genny walked into the bathroom. She didn't seem at all surprised or even a bit grossed out. "This happens to first time wishers a lot," she said. "You'll adapt and get used to it, you humans tend to get carried away at first, but you learn from the pain. That's why I let you do it!"

I staggered over to her. "You could have warned us."

Genny nodded. "Yes, I could have, but you wouldn't have learned anything from that. Experience is the best teacher!" She opened up her hand and showed me a big breath mint. "You better take this. You have terrible breath right now! I'm an immortal creature of immense power and your breath is making my eyes water."

The echo of Barry still barfing made it hard to hear so I walked back into Barry's bedroom. "Oh, my breath isn't that bad!" I told Genny.

Rover walked up to me. "I have to agree with the genie. I could smell your breath from across the room and it made me gag! And like you said, I like sniffing butts!"

"Come on!" I told Rover.

My breath hit Rover's nose. He gasped and rolled over on his back, playing dead. Putting my hand over my mouth, I said, "Oops, my bad." I popped the mint into my mouth. It tasted cool and fresh like peppermint. After breathing a little puff of air into my hand and sniffing it, I felt confident my breath could no longer knock out a dog.

I bent down to pet Rover. "Sorry buddy," I said.

Rover's eyes slid open just a bit. He shook his head. "Did you get the number of that truck that hit me?" he said.

I heard the toilet flush. Barry stumbled out of the bathroom. "Man, that wasn't fun!" he said.

Genny walked over to him and dropped a breath mint into his open mouth. Barry closed his mouth and smiled. "Yum, tasty!" He chewed the mint. "Thanks! I needed that!"

"How about some orange soda to wash it down?" Genny asked Barry.

His face lit up as he grabbed the bottle of soda. "Orange soda is my favorite, how did you know? What are you reading my mind?" Barry laughed.

CHAPTER FIVE
BARRY

Genny cocked her head. "I am your genie. I am here to fix problems for you. And first-time wishers always have problems."

"It wasn't a problem until we puked! All the cookies and pies were tasty!" Tammy said.

"But we learned from it!" I insisted. "We now know it's possible to get too much of a good thing!"

Genny smiled. "See you little humans learn fast!" Her smile grew. "Now what other problems can I help you with. Real problems?"

Tammy's face lit up. "Well now, there are these bullies in school. They love to push us around and make fun of us. I want to be able to teach them a lesson."

Rover spoke up. "You two both take karate lessons. You're green belts! You should be able to protect yourselves."

"Correct!" I said performing a snap kick.

"That's true," Tammy said. "But sensei says it will be years before we can really defend ourselves from a group of bullies. He says we should use our words to defend ourselves."

"He's a smart man!" Rover said. "There are no shortcuts in life."

"Maybe not real life, but with magic there is!" Genny said.

"Really?" Tammy leaned towards Genny.

"Would I lie to you?" Genny answered.

"That's not answering her question!" Rover said.

Genny put her arm around Tammy. "Girl, just say the word or words and you two are the world's greatest ninjas!"

"There are no such thing as ninjas!" Rover insisted.

Genny laughed. Her eyes twinkled. "Not yet there aren't, but just say the words!"

"I wish I was a ninja!" Tammy said.

"Me too! I wish I was a ninja too!" I didn't want to be left behind. Plus, if Tammy was a ninja, I would need to be one too, in case I had to defend myself against her.

Genny snapped her fingers. "Wish granted. You two are now both amazing ninjas!"

"I don't feel any different!" I said.

"Neither do I!" Tammy said.

Genny crossed her arms and frowned. "Really, after all I have done for you. You still don't trust me!"

"All you've done so far is get them sick!" Rover said.

"Not true," Genny said turning away from him. "I gave them unlimited sweets and now they're expert ninjas!"

"Ah, we don't feel like ninjas!" I said.

"Yeah, how do we know we're ninjas?" Tammy asked.

Genny held her arms in the air. She pulled them apart to reveal a warped window. "Here, doing is believing!" she said. As we looked through the window, a bunch of cats leapt towards us. Genny squeezed her arms together, squishing the window shut.

"Cats?" Tammy asked.

"Give it a second," Genny said, pointing at the cats.

The cats grew and grew. Their front legs became arms with hands. Swords appeared in their hands. Then light green, leathered armor grew over their bodies.

"Now they are ninja cats!" Genny declared proudly.

"You're kidding!" Tammy exclaimed nervously.

One of the cats flicked his wrist at Tammy, throwing his sword at her. Tammy swatted the sword away like nothing. She smiled. She took a fighting stance. "Oh, it's like Donkey Kong!" she said.

"Wait! Four against two. Is that fair?" I asked Genny.

Genny laughed. "No, it's not. I should have brought in more ninja cats, but your room is too small."

The cats spun their swords over their heads. "Ha, we have more than enough cat ninja power here to defeat you two puny humans!" one of them shouted.

The cat leapt up through the air doing somersaults towards me. I was very impressed by the move. But part of me, a part of me that I didn't know I had, told my brain to move to the side, which I did. As I slid to the side, the cat hit the ground right where I had been standing. That special part of my brain said "duck." So, I did and the cat's sword swung over my head. Without even thinking, I sprang up and hit the cat with a fist to its nose. The cat's head shot back. I dropped down and spun around, sweeping the cat's legs out from under him. He hit the ground super hard. A second cat ninja flew through the room at me with his sword extended. I simply stepped to the side and let his sword glide by me. I quickly trapped the cat's attack arm onto my side. Then, I hit the trapped cat with the most awesome jumping snap kick I had ever performed! The cat dropped both of his swords and his eyes popped open in disbelief. Yet, he refused to fall. I lightly tapped him on the forehead and down he went.

Turning to Tammy, I saw her standing victorious over her two cat ninjas. She pinned them down with one foot while flexing her muscles. "I could get used to this!" she said.

"See!" Genny said proudly. "I would have needed about ten more cat ninjas to make it a fair fight. But I figured this would prove my point." Genny snapped her fingers and the cats disappeared.

"Man, we are so awesome!" Tammy said.

I had to agree with my sis. I had never felt this strong, this powerful, this in control.

"Yeah, this is going to be fun!" I told Tammy.

"Is it?" Rover asked. "Is it?"

"Yes!" Tammy, Genny and I all said at once.

Genny smiled and yawned. "Now if you don't mind, this first day out of the tube after a few decades has got me all worn out. I need to retire to my tube to rest."

"Cool," I told her. "Rest is good."

"Just remember, when I am in the tube never close it. Or else your reign of wishes will be over!"

"Got it!" Tammy said.

"I got it too!" I agreed.

"I'm still not sure this is a good idea!" Rover said. He pointed to his eye with a paw and then pointed at Genny. "I got my eyes on you lady."

Genny smiled. She turned into gas form and floated into the bottle. From the bottle she called, "If you need me, just make a wish!"

CHAPTER SIX
TAMMY

The next day, Barry and I walked to school like always since it's only a couple blocks away from our house. It would seem extra lazy if we didn't walk. Besides, Mom would have to drive us if we didn't and she already worked so hard that Barry and I liked to give her a break in the morning. Of course, now that we had a genie, Barry and I could make Mom's life even easier. We just needed to figure out the best way to do it.

"Do you think Genny can still grant us wishes while she's at our home in her tube?" Barry asked.

I had to admit that wasn't a stupid question.

"Hey you kids!" Our neighbor, Mr. Powder, yelled at us from his front porch.

"Hey back at you!" Barry yelled to him while waving.

"Your dog better not poop on my yard again today!" Mr. Powder screamed.

"We will try to not let him!" Barry called back, smiling, then he turned to me. "I like him. He likes to keep his yard nice and clean. Now that Rover understands us, we can tell him not to poop there."

I rolled my eyes. It's amazing that twins could be so different. Only Barry could like a grumpy old grouch like Mr. Powder. Instead of wasting my time on Mr. Powder, I was thinking about possible wishes.

We made it to the school yard. For once, I felt really good about going to school. I always thought school was okay, but now that we had a genie, school would be better than okay. I just needed to figure out the best way to use Genny. Yesterday proved that magic was fun, but it could be tricky. I didn't want to tire her out with silly wishes.

No sooner did we get into the school than we heard Mo Brown call out to us. "Hey, Denton Geeks!"

I kept walking, ignoring him, but my dumb brother stopped and turned. "Hey Mo, what's up?" he asked.

Mo strutted over towards us. Of course, he had Ned and Fred Rock backing him up. Mo held out a giant hand to Barry.

"I need money!" he demanded.

Barry smiled at the big jerk. "Did you forget your money again?"

Mo shook his head. "Nah, I got mine. I need yours."

Barry looked Mo in the eyes. "Well, Mo I'd love to help you out, but I didn't bring any extra money. Sorry Pal!"

Mo put his hand on Barry's shoulder and squeezed it. "That's not my problem, bro!"

Barry, dense as always, didn't seem to notice he was being threatened. "Actually, Mo, it is. I don't want to hurt you, but I need my money for lunch," Barry said sternly. "Now please remove your hand from my shoulder!"

Well, well. I had to give Barry some credit; he did recognize a shake down when he saw one.

Mo stood up on his tiptoes and glared down at Barry. "Yeah, whatcha gonna do about it?" he taunted.

In one fast motion, Barry took Mo's hand, pulled it off his shoulder, twisted it backwards, and drove him to the ground. "I believe I will do this!"

Ned and Fred both lunged at Barry. "Hey, you can't do that to our buddy!" Fred said.

"Yeah!" Ned said.

They both curled their hands into fists.

Leaping through the air, I landed between the two big thugs and my brother. I blocked both of their punches. Then, I extended my arms and hit them both in the solar plexus. The two dudes doubled over and fell to the ground.

Man, that felt so good!

"What in the name of Sam Hill is going on here?" A loud voice called out from the other end of the hallway. It was Principal Phillips. He was a huge man, standing at least six and a half feet tall and he had to weigh over 300 pounds. He looked like a retired pro wrestler.

"Sir, it's not what it seems!" I told the big principal, who was rushing toward us.

He stood in front of me with his arms crossed. "Well Ms. Denton, I saw you take down the Rock boys with punches." He pointed to Barry holding Mo down. "I see your brother has Mo Brown in a wrist lock."

"Ah, okay, it is what it seems, but we have good reason!" I said. "They were trying to shake us down for money!"

"That's not true!" Mo said. "I have all the lunch money I need. And if you look I'm sure Barry has all of his money."

"Yeah because we stopped you!" I said. "We beat the snot out of you three!"

Principal Phillips stood with his muscular arms crossed. "You just admitted it to me." He pointed down the hall. "My office now!" he ordered.

We gulped.

CHAPTER SEVEN
BARRY

Principal Phillips led us to his office. I had never been there before. It was much smaller and cramped than I thought it would be. Pointing to two chairs in front of his desk, he ordered, "Sit down you two!"

I sat immediately. Tammy stayed standing. "Sir, we didn't do anything!" she insisted.

The big man crossed his arms and shook his head. "From what I saw you two did a lot," he told Tammy. "Look, I know the Rock boys and Mo can be a handful. But from what I saw, and that's all I can go by, you two beat them up. That's wrong on so many levels. Violence in the school is wrong."

An announcement came over the loud speaker. "Principal Phillips you are needed in room 222."

The big man sighed and mumbled, "It's going to be one of those days where I miss my fighting days of getting thrown to the matt and pounded on." Looking at us he said, "Stay!" Principal Phillips stormed out of the office.

"Hey, how are my groovy new friends doing?" Genny said, appearing on the Principal's desk.

"Nobody says groovy anymore," Tammy said.

"Are you sure?" Genny asked.

"Yes!" Tammy told her.

Genny slid off the desk and looked around the room. "Boy, I leave you two alone for a little bit and you get into trouble. You are just like my old magic mate Billy. That man couldn't do anything without me, until I made him really rich."

"Now, what can I do for you two? Want me to turn your principal into a worm. I like worms, they are quiet and help the ground. It's a win, win." Genny said.

"No," Tammy said. Her eyes popped opened. "Wait, you can do that?"

"Well, duh," Genny said.

"Duh, really? You really have been in that tube awhile. Nobody says duh anymore."" Tammy told her.

"Man, you people speak so boring these days. I blame cell phones, emojis, and selfies. I mean, come on, what's the big deal about taking pictures of yourself? I don't get it. Though I do bet my old friend Adonis would love it. But I digress," Genny said. "So, do I worm him?"

I looked at Tammy. From the way she eagerly rubbed her hands together I knew she was tempted. "We can't turn our principal into a worm. The man was just doing his job. We did beat up Mo, Ned and Fred and while that was awe-some it was also kind of wrong."

"No, it wasn't!" Tammy insisted. "Those jerks have picked on us for forever, all because they are bigger than us. They thought they had more power than us. It felt great to teach them a lesson!"

"Sounds like you used your power for good!" Genny said, floating up to the ceiling. She seemed to have a lot of nervous energy, which I kind of liked.

"Tammy, we still can't turn our principal into a worm. That's wrong!" I said.

Genny rolled her eyes. She actually acted a lot like Tammy did. "Well of course YOU can't turn him into a worm, but I can. You can use my power for your benefit."

Tammy groaned. "I hate to say this, but Barry might be right."

I started to make my point. But then realized that she had agreed with me. "Wait, you agree with me?"

Tammy exhaled. "Yes, it does look like we were the bullies here. We can't punish the principal for doing his crappy job."

"He's helping shape young minds!" Barry said.

Tammy pointed to Principal Phillips's desk. "Look at this, there's stuff everywhere in this office. This poor guy has to deal with lots of annoying students all the time."

Principal Phillips walked back into his office. "Sorry about the delay."

Genny pointed at the big man and he instantly froze in place. She floated down to the floor. "I think this poor man would enjoy being a worm. It'd take some of the pressure off of him."

"No, we can't do that," I said.

"How'd you freeze him like that?" Tammy asked.

"I'm in tune with whomever releases me from the tube. I sense that's what you wanted me to do. Right?" Genny said, touching Tammy on the shoulder.

Tammy nodded. "Yes, I did."

Genny smiled. "See, just pleasing you guys. It's what I do!" Her eyes widened. "It's far out! Right?"

"Nobody says that anymore either," Tammy told her.

"Man, the 2000s are so boring," Genny groaned. She tapped Principal Phillips on his chest a few times. "Okay, now how do we handle this? I don't like people punishing my kids. It cramps our style." She thought for a second and added, "It hurts our team dynamic." She smiled at us. "I'm glad you two have such high moral standards. We will do great things together!"

"Thanks!" I said.

"I'm all for team building!" Genny said. "I taught my last partner Billy G that. So now what do I do with the principal? He's not part of our team."

"Let's make him a fan of our team!" Tammy said.

"Oh, I like how you think!" Genny told her.

"Wait, what does that mean?" I asked.

Genny snapped her fingers. Principal Phillips started to move again. He smiled. I don't think I'd ever seen him smile before. "Oh, you two amazing kids just did the school a favor by putting those three bullies in their place." His smile grew even wider. His eyes popped open. "Oh, oh, oh! I have a great, amazing idea!" he said leaning right into us. "Why don't you fine, amazing, fantastic students take the day off?"

"But we have a history test today!" I said.

Principal Phillips gave us a little dismissive wave. "Don't worry about it. I'll talk to your teacher. You two both got A's!" He pointed outside. "Now go! Go have some fun!"

I should have said something. But truthfully, neither Tammy nor I had studied for the test. We were so excited about Genny that we had forgotten about our normal lives.

"Come on bro, let's go!" Tammy said.

"You lead the way, sis!" I told her. This was going to be fun! Tammy and I were free to do whatever we wanted! And we had Genny to help us!

CHAPTER EIGHT
TAMMY

Being free from school, Barry and I decided to go home and take Rover for a walk before we did anything really fun. After all, he was now a part of our magic team and we wanted to make sure he got some exercise. We wanted to keep him happy.

When we got home, we found Rover sleeping on the couch. He looked up when he heard us walk into the living room, "Is it three o'clock already?" He yawned. "Time flies when you are sleeping."

"It's only nine o'clock bud!" Barry said.

"Then why are you home? Did that Genny genie do something to get you kicked out of school?" He got up on all fours. "If she did, I will so bite her in the butt. I need my break from you kids!"

"No, she kind of, sort of, put Principal Phillips in our power ... so he gave us the day off!" Barry bragged.

Rover sighed. "I don't think that's better. Where is she now?"

I shrugged. "No idea. She's free to do what she wants as long as she keeps granting us our wishes."

"Wait, so that's all you think about? Just having your wishes granted?" Rover asked.

"Pretty much yeah," I said.

"I agree," Barry said. "We can now wish for a good present for Mom!"

Barry had a point. Now that the tube was open, we couldn't give that to Mom. We needed something new, something better.

"Genny!" I called out.

Genny appeared. "You rang?"

"We need to give my mom a great birthday gift!" I said.

Genny smiled and snapped her fingers. "Done! I got her the best thing she could possibly want. The thing she really needs. She just doesn't know it."

My phone rang. I looked at it. "It's Mom," I said, answering the call. "Hi Mom! You're on speaker."

"Kids, I'm sorry I missed you this morning. I had to go to work early to prepare for a presentation," Mom said.

"That's okay, Mom!" I said.

"Yes," Barry said. "We know you work hard!"

"Well, I just got a bit of weird, but great news. The University liked my presentation so much that they want me to go to Hawaii for the week for a conference. My boss was going to go, but now they are sending me. And they're paying for everything! They want me there so fast that I can't even stop home to pack and say goodbye. I talked to your Aunt Mary and she will check in with you every day. She says if you need anything she is of course just down the street and ready to help. But if you kids don't want me to go, just say the word."

"Go! We'll be fine," I told Mom. "We want you to be happy!"

"Yeah," Barry added. "We can handle ourselves. Plus, we have Rover here!"

Mom laughed. "Yes, I'm sure Rover is a lot of help!" A pause. "Are you sure you're okay with it?"

"Will you be home before your birthday on Sunday?" Barry asked.

"Of course!" Mom said.

"Then go for it!" Barry said.

"I love you two!" Mom said.

"We love you too!" I said.

"Ditto!" Barry said.

Mom hung up. Genny smiled. "Tada!"

"You really think sending Mom away for a few days was the perfect gift for her?"

"I gave your mom an all-expenses paid vacation. Plus, she will get a raise now. So yes, you've given her a great gift by letting her go!" Genny said. "Plus, you two are a lot of work, I'm sure she could use the pampering. She actually wanted your Aunt Mary to come stay with you but I used my convincing powers to change her mind. Mary would cramp our style and I'd end up turning her into a worm."

I actually couldn't find any flaws with what Genny said. Besides, it was probably a good thing that we didn't have to worry about Mom overhearing us talking to Rover and Genny. She'd probably think we were going whacko and try to talk me out of my plans for world domination.

"I don't like the way your mom laughed when she said she was sure I'd be a big help!" Rover said. "I am a big help! I bark at the door when random people come over. I wake you kids up so you can go to school. I give you guidance even though you don't listen! What more can I do?"

"Mom doesn't know you can talk," I told him.

"Still those other things are important too! Plus, I lick you guys clean sometimes! I really don't get enough credit for that!" Rover said.

"Sorry," I told him, patting him on the head.

"I still don't like the idea of you kids skipping school!" Rover said. "School is important!"

"You flunked out of obedience class!" I reminded him.

"That's because I didn't need that kind of training. I'm already the most obedient one in the house," Rover said.

"Maybe," Barry said.

"He even smells better than you most of the time," I told my bro.

"What do you mean most of the time?" Rover said. "All the time! Remember my nose is very sensitive." Rover looked at me. "I really think you kids should get back to school!"

"You know we could," I said. "Or we could take you for a walk!" I told him.

Rover's ears popped up. "A walk, a walk, walk!" He shouted, tail wagging. Yep, you could make the dog talk, but at the end of the day, he was still a dog.

CHAPTER NINE
BARRY

We put Rover on his favorite, long leash and headed out the door. It felt weird walking Rover in the morning on a school day since part of my brain figured that I should be in school, learning stuff. Yet another part of my brain was telling me to chill out and enjoy this lucky break. I wasn't sure which part of my brain I should listen to, but I knew which one I wanted to listen to.

"This feels great, but weird," I told Tammy.

"You're making less sense than normal," she responded. "This freedom is amazing!"

"I mean, I love being free and walking with Rover and you. But I also kind of, sort of, maybe feel like this is wrong. We should be in school now. Learning stuff. It's the responsible thing to do."

51

Tammy stopped walking. She glared at me. "Dude, this is something I don't say very often. Heck, I don't think I've ever said it. But you're thinking too much!"

"Is it possible to think too much when we have a magical genie who can grant us our every wish?" I asked.

Tammy nodded her head. "Yes!" she said. "We have a freaking genie that lets us do anything. She just gave Mom the vacation of a lifetime! She gave us the day off from school. Don't think too much about this!"

I hadn't noticed that we had stopped on Mr. Powder's sidewalk. Of course, he saw us and came running out of his house, shaking his fist. "Keep your dirty dog off of my lawn! I'm going to call the dog catcher! Or, I'll call the police!" Mr. Powder shouted.

"Man, that seems like a big overreaction to walking by the house with a dog," Rover said. "This guy has issues. No wonder why he lives alone."

Mr. Powder kept coming towards us with his fist shaking faster and faster.

Rover looked at him and added. "I know I'm not an expert on human fashion, but I don't get the sleeveless white t-shirt look. Unless the man wants to show off his armpit hair?"

"Why is your dog barking so insanely at me?" Mr. Powder demanded.

Oh right, he could only hear Rover's talking as barks. That was actually kind of cool, but it caused our angry neighbor to storm over to us.

Mr. Powder pulled an old cell phone from his pocket. It didn't seem much smaller than an ancient house telephone. He flipped the phone open and growled at us. "That's it. I'm calling the pound!"

"Ah, Mr. Powder sir," I said in my friendly debate team voice. "I'm pretty certain walking a dog by your house is not an offense. We have him on a leash, and we have a bag to pick up his poops."

"I'm not pooping in public!" Rover said sternly. "That is so undignified. I only do that in the privacy of our backyard."

Mr. Powder only heard a series of angry barks.

Pointing at Rover, he said, "That dog is mad!"

"More like angry," I said. "He says he likes to poop in private and won't poop on your nice grass." I added the last part to compliment Mr. Powder. I hoped that would calm him down.

Mr. Powder only got angrier. "How do you talk to a dog? Are you kids on drugs?"

Tammy rolled her eyes. "No of course not."

Mr. Powder wasn't listening to anything. "That explains why you are walking around on a school day!" He started pushing buttons on his phone. "I'm calling the police. They'll come for you."

I noticed he hadn't turned his phone on yet. Pointing at the phone, I said, "Sir, I think you need to turn on your phone before you can do that."

"Don't help him!" Tammy said.

"Does Spring City even have a dog catcher?" Rover asked.

"Keep that dog under control!" Mr. Powder ordered.

Tammy sighed. "We have him on a leash."

"He better not bite me!" Mr. Powder shouted.

"Please, I'd rather bite three-day old socks than him!" Rover said.

Mr. Powder started to shake and turn red. "That dog is vicious!"

"No, he's just opinionated," I said.

"You're not helping bro!" Tammy told me.

"Man, I wish Mr. Powder was nicer," I said, without meaning to make a wish.

Genny appeared. "Wish granted!" she said and snapped her fingers.

Mr. Powder's ranting changed into panting. Turning towards him, we saw he had been turned into a cute little beagle.

"Oops!" I said. "I didn't mean that!"

Genny smiled. "Wish granted." She repeated. "Now he's nicer and he understands dogs better!" She turned to Mr. Powder, the beagle. "Sit!" she ordered.

He sat.

"Turn him back!" I said.

"Why?" Tammy said. "He's much nicer this way!"

"I like him much more like this," Rover said.

"But I didn't mean to make that wish!" I said.

Genny rolled her eyes. "Rules are rules, dude. You make a wish, I grant the wish. That's how we roll."

"Okay, great. Now I wish he was back to being a human. Just make him a nicer human!" I said quickly.

Genny shook her head. "No can do. Once a wish is made it can't be unmade. That's section 4 line 13 in the wish agreement, which you both agreed to. Remember?"

"Look bro," Tammy said putting her arm around me. "This is better for him. The man was obviously angry and lonely. Now the dog catcher will find him and put him in the pound. He'll get a good home. He'll be happy!"

"But—," I said.

"Plus, I repeat there is no dog catcher!" Rover said.

Tammy shook her head. "No buts. We can't undo the wish so we just deal with it. Think of it this way, we learned an important lesson. We need to be careful with what we say!" she said with an evil grin on her face.

I hated to admit it, but Tammy was right. Man, Tammy was almost always right. Mr. Powder wasn't a great person. Maybe he would be a better dog. And we learned we would have to choose our words carefully.

"Okay, but from now on, we do things to help the world!" I said.

"Sure," Tammy said.

"Come on, let's get walking. I don't want to be around to see if there is a dog catcher in town," Rover said.

CHAPTER TEN
TAMMY

For the next few days Barry and I sat at home and practiced using Genny. We had her bring us pizza, wings, and tacos. We had her give us straight A's in all our classes. Oh, we also went to a Beyoncé concert that I wanted to see, and to a Paul McCartney concert Barry wanted to see. You know—average, fun things. I knew we could have done more, but I wanted to get the hang of using Genny's power. Anyway, we needed a couple of days off from school because we had to prepare for my city league soccer game and Barry's next debate.

As we sat in our living room playing video games on our new 100 inch, 4k TV, Rover lectured us. "I can't believe you two haven't gone to school all week!"

"Yeah, well, the idea of going to school is to get good grades. We already have straight A's thanks to Genny," I told him.

"No, no, no! The idea of going to school is to learn!" Rover insisted.

"I've learned having a genie is cool!" I said.

Rover pointed to our giant new TV. "How are you going to explain that new TV to your mom when she gets home? Huh? Huh?"

"We'll tell Mom we won it on an internet gift site. She'll believe that. We've even had Genny create the site on the internet. It's awesome!" I said.

"You kids are getting too dependent on Genny!" Rover warned.

"Nah, we're not," I said. "Besides we're going to school this afternoon. Barry has his debate team captain contest with Casey Mills and I have my soccer game against Maggie's team. Man, they're so going to go down." I laughed.

"Isn't Maggie's team undefeated?" Rover asked.

"Yeah, but I have Genny on my side now," I smiled.

Rover pointed at Barry, whose eyes were locked on the tv as his fingers glided over the joy stick. "How is Barry going to debate when he hasn't moved from that video game in hours?"

"Don't worry puppy," I said. "We've got magic on our side."

"That's exactly why I'm worried!" Rover said. "You've had magic for just a few days and you're already totally dependent on it."

I laughed at him. "No! I still go to the bathroom by myself." I stopped to think for a moment. "Maybe I can make it so—"

"No, no, no!" Rover shouted. "Don't even go there!"

"Oh fine," I told him. "But man, it would sure save some time." I sighed.

Rover pointed at the new 3D holographic clock on the wall. "Speaking of time, don't you think you should be getting to your game and your brother to his debate match?"

I stood up from our new super comfy, adjustable, heating and cooling couch with built in wifi. "That's a good point. See dog, you are still very useful to us!"

"Oh joy," Rover said. "I'm so glad that me, the dog, can be the unlikely voice of reason!"

Did Rover make any sense? Nah, what could go wrong?

CHAPTER ELEVEN
BARRY

It felt good being back at school again with my boys at the debate club. Sure, staying at home getting straight A's, eating great food, going to concerts, and playing video games was awesome. But, being in the auditorium with my debate team felt great in a different way. A more real way.

Bobby Lands came running up to me when he entered the auditorium. Bobby was a big, red headed kid that was my best friend, besides Tammy of course. He didn't have that twin's bond that Tammy and I had. Still, he understood me and loved debating just as much as I did.

"Dude, I've missed you these last couple of days!" Bobby told me.

"Yeah, my sis and I have been feeling a little off lately." I told him. "So, we stayed away from school. Just to be on the safe side!"

"Smart!" Bobby said patting me on the back.

Ms. Pitts, the debate club teacher rep, walked up to the podium. Her name wasn't really Ms. Pitts, we just called her that because the tall, lanky woman always had sweat stains under her arms.

There were five us on the debate team: Me, Bobby, Cindy Mills, Dan Decker and Cindy's brother, Casey. Casey happened to be my competition for debate team captain. He was a tall, blonde kid who was also captain of the baseball team, school president, and all-around popular guy. I really didn't know why he wanted to be debate club captain too. I guess he just liked being the man, the leader.

In any other area, I wouldn't have stood a chance against Casey, but debate was my thing. I knew I had my vote and Bobby's vote. All I needed to do was convince either Dan or Cindy to vote for me. Cindy may have been Casey's sister, but I always thought she had a thing for me. So I had a chance.

Ms. Pitts stood at the podium. She cleared her throat. "Barry and Bobby, please take you seats so we can begin."

Bobby and I walked to our seats. Mine was right next to Casey's. I noticed Genny hovering over us in the room. It gave me an extra boost of confidence.

Ms. Pitts explained the rules to us. "This is a debate-off to determine who will be named captain of this year's debate team." Everybody on the team clapped politely. Casey looked at me and snickered.

Ms. Pitts cleared her throat. She did that a lot. "The format of this event will be very simple. Each of our two candidates will stand up here, face their peers, and then tell us why they believe they should be leader of the debate team. They will have three minutes. Then their opponent may ask them one question." She paused to let that sink in. "Any questions?"

We all shook our heads no.

Ms. Pitts smiled. She cleared her throat and then said, "Casey, please come to the podium."

Casey stood up. I had forgotten how tall he was. Man, the kid had a lot of muscles. Well I guess he had the same number of muscles I had, but his were much bigger and more defined. He smiled. His teeth glistened. That's okay, I told myself. This was a debate, not a beauty contest.

I had this. Right? I looked up at Genny, who was smiling at Casey as he took the podium. "Friends and teammates on the debate team. I am sure that my friend Barry is a worthy debater. He is a great asset to the team. He works hard and always contributes. But is Barry a leader? I don't think so." He paused for a moment, then continued. "But do any of you question my ability to lead?" He paused again.

I found myself shaking my head no. It seemed like everybody else on the team also shook their heads no. Even Ms. Pitts and Genny shook their heads.

"Now, I know how to lead. I led the baseball team to its first state championship. I am school president and lead my class in GPA. Do you all agree I am a leader?"

Looking at everybody else in the room, they all were nodding yes. I had to fight the urge to nod yes, too. Man, the kid was good.

"Then please give me the honor of leading you to victory in debate!" Casey said.

Ms. Pitts started clapping. "Very good, Casey. Very good." She suddenly remembered me. "Oh! Barry, do you have a question for Casey?"

I stood up. I thought I had a clever question for him. "So Casey, why does a guy like you want to lead the debate team? After all, you're a cool kid and cool kids don't usually like debate."

Casey smiled at me. "Excellent question, Barry. While I agree that I am a cool kid, I think all of you are also cool kids. It's a cool thing to debate and show the world how intelligent you are. As your debate team captain, I can help you and the others win and show the world how cool you are!"

Wow! Casey was good. Even I was seriously considering voting for him. I took a deep breath. No, not going to happen. Sure, Casey was smart and handsome and made a good point or two, but this was my thing. I had been preparing for this all my life. Well, except for the last few days when I let my concentration slip some. But, I had this.

I walked up to the podium. My pits were sweating. Now I knew how Ms. Pitts felt. I stood there in front of everyone. I opened my mouth, wanting to say inspirational words, instead the words: "Ah, ah, ah, ah oh hi," rolled off my tongue. Okay, they didn't exactly roll, more like they fell off my tongue. Not the best start, but I could save this. A good debater never gives up. I cleared my throat. "Sorry, about that," I told the others. "I guess my throat was a little dry. You know why it was so dry? It's because I thirst to lead this team!" I said while looking at their faces. Bobby cracked a little smile. The others just looked at me. "I know Casey is a great leader, a natural leader," I said. Oh man, I thought to myself: I just told everybody Casey is great. That might have not been the best move. I wish I could take that back.

Time flashed before me like I was rewinding a video. I saw myself and heard the words:

redael larutan a, redael taerg a si yesaC, come backwards out of my mouth. Everything went silent. I was back a few seconds in time. *Hey, I didn't wish that out loud*, I thought.

"*I know,*" I heard Genny say in my head. "*I can now grant your thought wishes. It's a great time saving move!*"

"Ah, Barry you're supposed to keep talking," Ms. Pitts told me.

"Right!" I said. "I've been doing debate my entire life. I live for debate. I love debate." I glanced at the faces of my teammates. They didn't look at me nearly the same way they had looked at Casey.

Oh, crud. I wished they loved me, I thought.

Their faces all turned to smiles. They all stood up and started clapping and throwing me kisses.

"Yeah Barry, you rock!" one of them shouted.

"Barry, I love you!" Cindy said.

Ms. Pitts jumped up and down eagerly. "Barry, you were amazing!"

The entire team surrounded me and started patting me on the back.

"*See isn't it great that I can answer your thought wishes?*" Genny said in my head.

CHAPTER TWELVE
TAMMY

I did my leg stretches on the soccer field. I knew my latest ninja skills would be a big asset to me now. After all, having the coordination of a ninja had to make me a better soccer player. Plus, I had Genny on my side. I had this. Heck, this would just be the beginning. This was going to be the year of Tammy! Two of my teammates, Karen and Lori Green, came over to me. They smiled. "Boy we're glad you made it, Tammy!" Karen said.

"Of course I made it. I love soccer," I said.

"Yeah but you haven't been in school for a couple of days. We thought you might be sick," Lori said.

I nodded to them. "I had something to take care of at home. But trust me, everything is great. I'm going to love beating Maggie's team!"

Karen and Lori looked at me. "That would be amazing. But her team is undefeated. Maggie scores like two goals every game," Karen said.

Lori nodded. "Yeah, she may be mean, but she's a darn good soccer player!"

"We're good, too!" I told them.

"We've only won one game," Karen said.

"And that was by forfeit," Lori added.

Flexing my muscles, I said, "I got this!"

The ref blew the whistle for us to come to the center of the field. Once we all got there, he gave us a speech. "Okay, kids I want a good clean game."

"Don't worry, my team is going to clean the field with them!" Maggie joked.

A couple of girls on her team laughed, while the girls from my team gulped. The ref rolled his eyes. He dropped the ball in the middle of the field, blew his whistle and yelled, "Play!"

Maggie immediately took control of the ball. Dribbling down the field, she darted between two of our defenders. I raced after her, making it my mission in life to stop her. No way was Maggie going to get the best of me! While chasing her down, I saw Genny in a red cheerleader uniform rooting for me. I could hear her chanting: "Go Tammy! Go Tammy! Go Tammy!"

It wasn't the most original cheer, but I did seem to speed up with each word. I passed Maggie and stole the ball from her.

"What the heck," she spat. "Where did you come from?"

Turning back over my shoulder, I gave her a taunting wink. Now in control of the ball, I worked my way up the field. I ran past a couple of defenders and lined up for the goal. The goalie came out to cut down my angle. I moved my head one way, then kicked the ball the opposite way. The goalie was completely faked out and the ball flew into the goal!

My team exploded with applause. They all ran up to me and slapped me on the back. I liked that. I liked that a lot.

Maggie and her team didn't like it though. They stood across the field, throwing darts at me with their eyes. I waved.

The ref blew the whistle. Maggie took the ball and charged up the field towards us. I was totally up for the challenge and told my team, "I got this!"

I ran towards Maggie. She yelled, "Come on Tammy, let's see what you got!"

Reaching down with my foot, I kicked the ball between Maggie's legs.

"What the …?" she shouted.

Using my ninja skills, I leapt over Maggie, landing right next to the ball. Dribbling back down the field, I kicked the ball into the net again. My team exploded!

Karen and Lori came running up to me. "Wow, you are awesome!" Karen said.

"Agreed!" Lori said. "I've never seen anybody do that to Maggie."

"I'm on my 'A' game!" I told them, looking up at Genny, who was giving me a thumbs up.

Karen leaned on my shoulder, pointing at Maggie and her team huddling together. "I don't like the looks of that. Maggie hates to lose and those girls hate to make Maggie mad. Be careful Tammy, they may come after you. Rec girls' soccer can be a vicious game. At least when Maggie plays!"

I laughed. "Don't worry, I got this!"

I hoped I could back it up. I wanted to wish to be the strongest girl in the world, but I didn't think I needed to be that strong to beat Maggie.

"Wish granted!" I heard Genny say in my head.

Looking up at Genny I thought, *I didn't make that wish!*

Genny floated there with her arms crossed. "You thought it," she said. "That's enough. I would've thought being a ninja would be enough for you, but if you want to be super strong too, that's cool!"

"But wait," I said.

69

While I was mentally debating with Genny, the game had continued. Maggie and her team had the ball and were determined to run me over and score. As Maggie dribbled the ball up the field, she was escorted by Pam Pouser, the biggest girl on their team. A rumor in school was circulating that professional wrestling companies were already recruiting Pam. She charged at me like an angry bull.

Being caught totally off guard, my ninja skills really couldn't come into play. Pam lowered her shoulder and plowed into me, but I didn't budge an inch. Pam, on the other hand, crumbled to the ground. Looking down at her now unconscious body, I said, "Oops, sorry about that!" But I really wasn't sorry. Pam had tried to take me out, so she got what she deserved.

Maggie still had the ball and was heading for our goal. I streaked down the field and landed in front of her.

"What? How?" Maggie said.

Tapping Maggie gently on the forehead, she collapsed to the ground. I smiled and took control of the ball. I had to be fifty yards from the goal. I figured, "what the heck?" I wound up and blasted the ball through the air. It went flying into the goal and actually broke through the netting.

"Yes!" I shouted, lifting my arms in victory!

I heard other people mutter, "Oh my!"

"The stench."

"The raw power."

Everybody else on the field fell to the ground holding their throats.

I sniffed myself. "What the?" I said. "I don't smell that bad!"

"Well not to you, cause you're super, but to normal people you are so strong that a whiff of your underarms will knock them out cold!" Genny smiled. "Cool, right?"

I locked my arms down to my side. "No! No, it's not!" I liked being able to easily overpower a crowd of people, but there had to be a better way than super B-O!

I saw Barry coming towards me, followed by a crowd of people who seemed to be hanging on his every word.

Oh my, things may have been getting out of control. But I kind of liked it!

CHAPTER THIRTEEN
BARRY

As I ran to the soccer field, I saw all of the people scattered on the ground. I quickly realized that Tammy wasn't having any more luck with Genny than I was. In fact, I felt pretty confident she was having a weird time too.

My new fans followed me over to Tammy. I felt like a mother duck with her ducklings. In a way, it was cool to have these people following me around, but it was also kind of creepy.

"What happened here?" I asked Tammy.

Tammy lifted up her arm. The smell knocked me over. "Never mind, I get it!" I said.

Genny smiled. "She wanted strength. I gave her strength!"

Tammy sighed and pointed at my new followers, "What's going on there?"

I smiled, feeling proud. "Genny made me very popular!"

Cindy grabbed my arm and leaned into me. "And we've never been happier!" The others behind Cindy all nodded in agreement.

Ms. Pitts looked at all the people laying on the field and said. "Dang girl, you stink more than I do!" She grinned. "Man, I wish I had that kind of power! Then I could finally live my dream of being a pro-boxer."

"Trust me, it's not a dream come true!" Tammy said.

"We need to get home and out of the public eye so we can figure out how to deal with this," I said, actually taking charge and liking it. Pointing at Genny, I said, "Take us to our living room. Do not change time or anything else. Just move us from here to there. And by us, I mean Tammy and me."

Genny smiled. "Oh, you are learning!" She snapped her fingers.

We appeared in our living room. Rover, who had been sleeping on the couch, popped an eye open. "Okay, what did you kids do wrong now?"

"Why do you assume we did something wrong?" Tammy asked him, her arms locked at her sides.

Rover said, "History. Plus you are holding your arms at your side like you have super B-O."

Tammy lowered her head.

Rover lifted his nose and rolled his eyes. "O-M-G, you do have super B-O."

Tammy sighed.

Rover looked at me. "What's your thing?"

"People do whatever I tell them," I said.

Rover pointed upstairs with his nose. "Tammy, you go take a shower. As for you Barry, avoid people until we figure out what to do." Rover rolled off the couch.

Rover sniffed the air. He looked at me. "Where is Genny now?"

I looked around then shrugged when I couldn't find her. "No idea."

He sniffed the air again. "Oh, no," he groaned. He walked over to the window. He shook his head. "This isn't right."

Following him to the window, I asked, "What isn't right?"

Rover pointed in the direction of Mr. Powder's house. Well, where Mr. Powder's house used to be. The house had been replaced by a tall, elegant mansion that glittered as if it were made out of gold.

"Oh, that can't be good," I groaned. "I wonder whose house that is now. I certainly don't think it's Mr. Powder's."

Rover rolled his eyes at me. "No, Mr. Powder is still the dog in the front yard."

I heard a knock at the door. "I wonder if that's Genny." I asked.

Rover rolled his eyes at me again. "Have you ever known that evil genie to knock?" he asked as I walked towards the door.

"No, but there's a first time for everything!" I noted.

As I opened the door, I saw Kate, the lady from the Used Antique Shop standing there.

"You know I can read minds," Kate told me.

"Ah, hi," I said.

Kate walked into the house. "You and your sister worked faster than I thought. I knew you'd be greedy and unleash the full power of the genie. But wow, you did it in just a few days."

"Actually, I'm surprised it took that long," Rover said.

Kate looked at Rover. She didn't seem taken aback by a talking dog. "Now, this a new one."

"I like to consider myself the voice of reason," Rover said proudly.

Kate bent down and petted Rover. "I bet you are!" she said.

"I told them to be careful with what they wished for. But nobody ever listens to the dog. We know things!" Rover said.

Kate nodded. "Yep and now she's free."

"What do you mean free?" I asked Kate.

"I don't want to explain this twice," Kate said. "Where's your sister?"

"Wait, why don't you obey my commands?" I asked. "Everybody else I talk to does whatever I say."

Kate laughed. "I'm not like everybody else!" she said. "I'm a gypsy queen. My job is to keep Genny contained."

Tammy came down the stairs with a towel around her head. "Well, you're not doing a very good job of it!" she said.

Kate smiled at Tammy. "Actually, I am. I needed you to overuse Genny's powers. She's free now. But at least when we catch her again she'll be worn out and won't be a threat for another thousand years or so. I'll be way old by then." Kate sniffed the air. "Wow, lots of soap and deodorant there, Tammy. I'm guessing she gave you super strength that gave you super B-O?"

Tammy stopped walking down the stairs. "Ah, maybe." A pause. "I like to think everybody fainted because I smelled so good."

Kate nodded. "Yeah, well whatever. But now that the Genie is literally out of the tube, we need get her back in."

"We'll just order her back in," I said. "But then, we'll have to forfeit the rest of our wishes. I guess that's ok, I'm pretty wished out."

"Me too," Tammy said.

Now Kate shook her head. "Like I said, it won't be that easy now." She pointed at the golden mansion next to our house. A neon hologram spun over the house that read: Home of Genny, Soon to Be Queen of the World.

"Oh, that can't be good," I sighed.

"I give Genny credit, the girl has confidence!" Kate said. "But that's also her weakness. The girl has such powerful magic that she never really bothers to think a lot. We have to outsmart her."

CHAPTER FOURTEEN
TAMMY

Kate, Rover and I sat around the dining room table trying to come up with a plan to stop Genny. As I gazed out the window, I saw police cars and everyday people lining up outside of her new mansion. They were all chanting, "We love Genny! We love Genny!"

Looking at Kate I said, "How could you let this happen? Why did you let us have Genny? Didn't you know she'd take over the town?"

Kate frowned. "Oh, the town is just the start. Soon it will be the state, then the country, then the world."

"Ah, that's worse," I pointed out.

"I am aware," Kate said. "That's why we have to stop her here and now."

"How?" I asked.

"We steal her power from her, pop her back into the test tube and seal her up for another thousand years," Kate said.

"How do we go about doing that?" Rover asked.

Kate grinned. "The first time I met your mom I knew she would have kids who would be capable of stopping Genny. That's why I made her my roommate. That's why I moved to this town—to keep an eye on you two."

"Oh, that's not creepy at all," I told her.

"I think it's a little creepy!" Barry said.

I rolled my eyes at my bro.

"It's actually an amazing honor," Kate insisted. "Meeting your mother, I realized that her children could possess the power to contain the magic."

Rover scratched himself. "You sure about that? So far these two have done nothing but let the magic go wild."

"They made you talk," Kate said. "You seem like a wise part of their team."

Rover nodded. "True, they did one thing right. But Barry talks to people and they fall in love with him. If Tammy works up a sweat and lifts her arms, she drops everybody around her."

Kate smiled. "Like I said, they are built to handle this amazing power. Plus, they've learned the downside of power so they will gladly give it back."

"Yeah," Barry said. "I'm not smart enough to have this kind of power."

Kate looked at him. "The fact that you realize that makes you smarter than most." She turned to me. "And your thoughts, Tammy?"

"I don't like lifting my arms and knocking out my team," I said. But I'm not gonna lie, I did kind of enjoy the power. But, I didn't want people to be scared of me. Plus, super B-O was very embarrassing. Being a ninja was kind of cool though, and the raw power from Genny made me feel amazing.

"Why are you smiling?" Rover asked me.

"I'm not." I shook my head in denial, but I could feel my mouth had been smiling.

Barry pointed at me. "You are!" he said.

"I just had gas," I said.

"Oh, that makes sense," Barry said. "I always feel better after a fart." His eyebrow popped up. "Wait! I didn't hear a fart."

"Okay, I kind of liked the idea of being super," I admitted. "But trust me. I'm over it. I want to go back to normal," I lied.

"Fair enough," Barry said.

Kate sat there, arms crossed. "I want to believe you," she said.

"Trust me," I said, faking sincerity. "I know my place in the world and it's not on top. I'm not ready for that." I had to admit I was torn.

Rover sniffed me. He turned to Kate. "I believe her. Tammy is impetuous and reacts before thinking, but she figures out her mistakes quickly."

Kate sat there, looking me in the eyes. "Well, you were chosen for a reason. I trust you."

"Thanks," I said, though Kate still creeped me out some. "How do we stop Genny?" I asked.

Barry laughed at me. "She told us, sis. We drain the power from her."

"But how do we do that?" I asked. "I'm pretty sure she won't just give us the power."

Barry thought about what I had said. "Oh, that's a good point." He turned to Kate. "How do we do it?"

"Very carefully," Kate said.

"I hope there's more to it than that," Rover said.

"There is. I just don't want to tip my hand too much," Kate said. "For now, you need to go over to her new place and draw her back over here. And bring the test tube back, too. The only way you can defeat her is to bring her back to the original spot where you opened the test tube. She's actually at her weakest there. She

81

can't break the tube. It's the only thing in the Universe that can contain her. The tube is what gives her power. But if sealed, it's the one thing on Earth that can hold her." She paused for a moment. "You must bring her back here, where you are the strongest."

"How do we draw her over here?" I asked. "She's not stupid. She won't just walk into a trap."

Kate smiled. "Like I said, the tube is a double-edged sword. It gives her power, but it can also contain her. The ancient ones so loved to be clever like that."

"Where would she keep the test tube?" Barry asked.

Kate frowned. "Somewhere nearby. She needs to hold it now and then. Maybe in her bedroom."

Great! We had to find a way to get into her bedroom and get her back here—all without tipping our hand. This would take all my skills!

CHAPTER FIFTEEN
BARRY

"Here's the deal," I told Kate and Tammy. "Rover and I will sneak over to Genny's house, slip past the guards, break in, find the bedroom, grab the test tube, and come back here. Then, on our home turf, Tammy will claim Genny's power and put Genny and the power back into the bottle. That'll be it, the day will be saved."

"Why are you going alone?" Tammy asked me.

"I'm not alone, I have Rover!" I said.

"Why are you bringing me?" Rover said. "I'm a freaking dog."

"Okay, Tammy, I'm not bringing you because, as I stated before, this job requires stealth and blending in. Something I'm very good at. Like when I don't want a teacher to call on me, I know how to sink down into my desk so they can't see me."

Tammy nodded. "You are good at that."

"Plus, we want you to battle Genny here, where you have the most power!" I added. "Plus again, you do have super B-O. That would make you stand out."

Tammy smiled. A smile that for some reason sent shivers down my spine. Had to be jitters from what was about to happen. Right?

"Why me?" Rover asked again. "Just to remind you—I am a dog."

I looked him in the eyes. "Your animal instincts should be able to warn me if I'm about to be caught. We can use those to our advantage."

Rover nodded. "That is true."

I looked at my sis and Kate. "You guys on board with this?"

Kate nodded her head. "Yes."

Tammy crossed her arms. "I guess," she sighed.

"Great!" I said with a huge smile. I loved this plan. I started towards the door and looked over my shoulder at Rover, who I coaxed. "Come on, boy."

Rover looked at me and sighed, too. "I suppose somebody has to keep you out of trouble!"

"That's the spirit!" I said.

Using the trees for cover, I darted out of the house. Due to my ninja speed, I moved too fast for normal eyes to detect. It felt so cool. A mob of people, mainly our neighbors, had flocked outside of Genny's new home. They all chanted, "We love you Genny!" over and over again.

A giant golden fence blocked my access to the mansion. Not only that, but the grounds were patrolled by what seemed to be the entire police force and the National Guard.

The easy part of this was fitting in with Genny's crowd of fans, or minions, or whatever. I simply walked with them, chanting, "Genny is great! Genny is awesome!" I made it to the front of the gate in no time. But her house was heavily guarded here. Leaping over the gate with my ninja skills would have caused a stir, so I worked my way to one of the side gates. There were not as many people there.

The grounds had so much security that it seemed Genny liked to be adored from afar. Either that, or she wanted to keep me and Tammy out. I could jump over and fight the guards, but then I would have lost the element of surprise that I was aiming for. Instead, I decided to see if my charm worked on controlled people.

Walking up to a few members of the mob waiting outside for Genny, I suggested, "Hey peeps, you know Genny would probably really love it if you showed your admiration for her by charging the fence and demanding to get in!"

Those who could hear me all nodded in acknowledgement. "This handsome lad makes total sense!" one woman said.

"Yeah!" another man shouted.

The group raised their hands and charged at the fence. "We want Genny! We want Genny!" they screamed. As the crowd hit the fence, the guards moved to stop them, leaving an area unmanned. I grinned. My plan was working.

"That was actually a good idea!" Rover said to me.

Picking up Rover, I hurried to the far end of the fence. Taking a deep breath, I leapt over the fence in one try with Rover in my arms. I landed squarely on two feet. I felt impressed with myself. But before I could pat myself on the back, two guards who were still on patrol, rushed over to me. They pointed tasers at me and yelled, "Halt!"

The two guards, a fat one and a short one, came at me slowly. "How'd you get in here?" one of them asked.

I shrugged. "I just jumped over the fence."

"Holding a dog?" the other guard asked.

I nodded. "Yep, he's a big Genny fan too! But he can't jump over a fence."

"Woof!" Rover said.

The guards looked confused. "We don't believe that you leapt over that fence!" one of them said.

Bending my knees, I leapt up through the air somersaulting towards the guards. I landed behind them. "Now do you believe it?"

The two nodded. "Get over here, you're under arrest." They rushed towards me.

I held a hand up. "I feel obligated to warn you two that I am an expert ninja."

The two stopped and pointed their tasers at me again.

"You probably shouldn't have told them that!" Rover told me.

"Ninja code of honor!" I insisted, never taking my eyes off of their trigger fingers.

They both pressed the triggers. I leapt into the air, jumping over their taser bolts. I landed behind the two security officers and gave them each a nerve punch. They both crumbled to the ground.

"Being a ninja is cool!" I moved forward, hiding in the shadows while getting closer to the mansion.

Slinking towards the back door, I saw two more guards patrolling the area by the mansion. I figured disabling them or even charming them might create more attention than I wanted. Instead, I picked up a rock and threw it over their heads. They heard the sound and ran towards it.

I had to move quickly so I rushed to the door, but it didn't open.

"Darn, it's locked," I whispered to Rover.

"You're a freaking ninja, pick the lock!" he told me.

"Can I do that?" I asked.

Rover just rolled his eyes at me. "Try!" he ordered.

"Right!" I said. I flicked my finger and my fingernail popped out. "Oh cool!" I said, sticking the extended fingernail in the door's lock. I jiggled it around until the door opened. "Ninja skills are awesome!" I slid past the door into a long, golden hallway.

Rover sniffed the air. "Let me lead the way!" he said.

Rover stopped and sniffed the air again. "Wait, I don't think we need to find the bedroom."

"What do you mean?" I asked.

"I'm right here fool!" Genny's voice was coming from behind me.

This was bad. I turned and saw Genny standing there, holding the test tube. She dangled it between her fingers. "You looking for this?"

"Yes," I said.

Rover rolled his eyes, "Dude, she knows that. She's taunting you."

"That's not polite!" I told her.

Genny laughed, smoke came out of her ears, and her eyes turned blood red. "You think taunting you is bad. Wait until I win once and for all by turning you into a little worm and squishing you!"

"Do your worst!" Rover growled.

"Dude," I told Rover softly. "Let's not make the crazy genie angrier."

Rover snickered. "I'm not scared of her!"

Genny crossed her arms. "You're in trouble now!" She blinked her eyes at me.

I didn't feel like a worm. Genny seemed to be on the same level as me. I thought if I was a worm I'd be shorter and looking up. Heck, if I was a worm I didn't think I'd have any eyes. "So far, being a worm is just like being a kid!" I said.

"That's because she can't worm you or do anything else bad to you!" Rover laughed. "Silly genie didn't even read her own contract. Genies can't do harmful magic on the owner or owners of the tube. She might have stolen it, but you and Tammy are still the true owners."

"Wow, nobody really does read those things!" I said.

Genie stomped toward me, smashing the floor with her feet as she drew nearer. "I'm a genie!" she roared. "I don't need any stinking magic to take you out, little boy!"

I calmly held my ground. Ninjas do not panic. It's not the ninja way. In fact, I extended my right hand, motioning for her to come at me.

"You seem pretty confident!" she laughed. Genny grabbed me and lifted me off the ground. "Over confident, I might say!" she laughed.

I head-butted her on the forehead. She screamed and dropped me to the ground, leaving her mid-section wide open. I hit her with a palm strike to the gut. My blow sent her reeling backwards. She hit a side wall so hard that it put a crack in it. She laughed. Okay, that was not the reaction I had been expecting.

"Oh, the ninja boy wants to play tough!"

Taking a fighting stance, I puffed out my chest and told her, "I haven't yet begun to fight!"

Genny drew a deep breath in. Her muscles started growing and popping out. She looked like a cartoon body builder. "I haven't begun to fight either!" she laughed. She started stomping towards me again. Each step shook the mansion.

Rover stood up on his back legs. He whispered to me. "You know you can't beat her like this. We need to get her back to the house."

Genny shot across the hallway. She hit me with an upper cut to my chin. The force of the blow sent me flying up to the ceiling and then crashing down to the floor. It stung a little, but not nearly as much as I thought it would have. I guess my ninja skills deflected a lot of the force. But I stayed on the ground, face first, pretending to be knocked out.

"Ha, foolish boy!" Ginny said, drawing closer to me.

I could hear her footsteps. Heck, you didn't need ninja skills to hear them. They sounded like a herd of rhinos. As she drew near me, I leapt up and jabbed her in the nose.

"Why you little brat!" she said. "That hurt somewhat, but not nearly enough to stop me!"

I showed her the test tube that I had ninja nabbed from her without her noticing. I waved it at her. "But I got this and with it, we can hurt you! Kate has a spell that will destroy you!" I said, hoping she didn't know I was bluffing.

Genny clenched her fist and turned bright red. And then, she grew and grew. She burst through the ceiling. She was angry, screaming, "Give it back!"

"I suggest we run!" Rover said.

"Yeah, good plan!"

I turned and leapt outside. I hit the ground running. I zigged and zagged through the crowds to our house. Looking over my shoulder, I saw Genny stomping through her mansion. It crumbled to the ground with her every step. She chased after me. But her followers got in the way, grabbing her legs and clamoring, "Oh Master Genny, what can we do for you?"

Genny ran over them, literally turning them into to toe jam.

"Oh gross!" I gulped. Turning tail, I ran and tumbled towards my house as fast as I could. I was panicked. I waved my hands and yelled, "She's coming! She's coming!"

Tammy opened up the door. "Yeah, we see that!"

"Are we ready?" I asked, darting into the house while waving the test tube in the air.

"We better be, since you brought her right here!" Tammy said.

"I thought that was the idea!" I said.

"It was. You did good, Barry!" Kate told me. She held out her hands. "Now give me the test tube!"

I handed her the test tube as I was told.

"Now what?" I asked.

"We make magic!" Kate smiled and pointed upstairs. "To your room!"

We ran up the stairs. The entire house shook. We reached my room just in time to see a giant Genny who had ripped the front of our house off. Her giant face peered into my room. "Give me that test tube!" she screamed.

"Okay, sis you're on!" I said.

CHAPTER SIXTEEN
TAMMY

Genny's giant head made me laugh. "Look lady, just because you're big, that doesn't mean you scare me. My brother might be a super charming ninja, but I'm a freaking super hero!" I shouted at her.

To prove my point, I flew through the air at her. I grabbed her ponytail and lifted her off the ground. I spun her around and around, then flung her in the air as hard as I could. She was headed toward space.

"Wow! I think you threw her into the ionosphere," Barry told me.

"Nerd!" I told him. I brushed my hands together. "That was easier than I thought!"

Barry pointed up. I saw something flying back down towards us. "Ah, I think it's going to take more than that to stop Genny."

"But, you admit that my move was impressive!" I said.

"Yeah, but you understand it's going to take more," Barry told me.

Genny came crashing down to the ground. She was even bigger now, probably close to fifty feet tall. "Ha! Was that all you got little girl?" she screamed.

I moved back into our original location—Barry's bedroom and looked at Kate. "You have a plan, right?"

"Yes, I do," Kate said. "I've been planning for this for a long time!"

I stood in front of Kate and Barry as Genny stormed towards the room, shaking the very earth itself. When she reached the house, she shrunk herself down to about ten feet tall, but she had razor-sharp claws and her eyes were burning red.

"Give me the test tube!" she bellowed in a voice that shattered the windows. Truthfully, it rattled me a bit, but I held my ground. I didn't want to seem scared.

In fact to hide my fear, I mustered up a laugh. "Ha! Is that the best you got?" I mocked. Dealing with Maggie and other mean girls had taught me to never back down. "I've seen scarier beasts in kid's shows!" I added. "PG-13 ones!"

"I will tear you both limb from limb and enjoy it!" Genny shouted as she stomped towards us.

"You can't hurt us, it's in the rules!" I said.

Stomping a foot down she screamed, "I changed the rules!!" She stopped, smiled sweetly with sweat beading on her brow. "So, if you are smart little children, you'll give me the test tube and declare me the rightful owner. Then I will let you live. Maybe I'll l even give you a small part of Earth to rule over. I can sense you enjoy power. Don't you, Tammy?"

My ears perked up at that idea. That didn't sound so bad. Our own little place on Earth to rule over. I did enjoy the power.

"Don't even think about that!" Barry screamed. "These types of deals never work out!"

"Right. Be strong!" Kate said. "We got her on the run! She's scared."

"She doesn't seem all that scared," I said. "Okay, Kate how do we get the genie back in the bottle?"

"This is where it gets tricky. Only you two can figure out this part. You have to get near to her, then draw her magical energy into you," Kate said.

"That doesn't sound too hard at all!" I said.

Leaping into the air, I extended my fist and flew at Genny at super speed.

Genny held her ground. At first, I thought it was because I was moving so fast that she couldn't see me. But no. My flight at her came to an abrupt halt when she reached out her hand and grabbed me by the throat. She lifted me into the air and squeezed.

Genny laughed. "Silly little human girl. I gave you your power, your strength. But it is only a small part of the strength I have. Thanks to your greed and ambition, I've grown so strong now! I can crush you like an ant."

Barry somersaulted towards us. The boy loved doing his somersaults. "Don't listen to her, sis," he coached. "She's scared of you! She's bluffing!"

"I am not!" Genny laughed, shaking me in the air. "Feel my grip! Does this seem like a bluff! I am the most powerful being on Earth now. You are like an annoying little insect to me. I will crush you and then crush all of you."

BAM! Barry threw a smoke bomb. Smoke filled the room.

Genny started to cough on the smoke, releasing her grip on me.

"See sis, she's not all that!" Barry said.

"Barry, nobody says that anymore!" I told him, rolling my eyes.

"Doesn't matter—we have her on the defensive now!" Barry shouted.

Genny shook her head. Her eyes cleared. They turned blood red. "No, you just made me mad!" she shouted.

Genny locked her glare on me. She leaned her face into mine. "Do you really think YOU can stop me?"

Lifting my arm, I pointed my armpit right at her nose. "Live by the magic, die by the magic!" I shouted, hitting Genny with a massive shot of super B-O!

Genny tried to hold her nose and cover her eyes at the same time. "Oh, that stinks!" she gasped.

Now was my chance.

"Back into the tube, genie!"

"No!" Genny screamed, "I have too much power! I won't go!"

"Come on, sis, pull that power from her!" Barry said.

I took a deep breath to clear my mind. I placed my index finger on Genny's forehead. "Get ready to let your power go and flow into me!" I ordered. I felt some of Genny's amazing power flowing into me, into my brain, igniting all of my cells.

"Never!" Genny shouted.

The flow stopped.

Rover leapt at Genny, biting her ankle.

"Ouch! You bratty dog!" Genny shouted, shaking her fist at Rover, "I'm going to—"

Inhaling, I pulled the last of Genny's power from her. I let the power course through me. It felt amazing like every cell in my body was awakened with white energy. I couldn't stop a full smile from appearing on my face. Flicking my finger, I tossed Genny back into her test tube.

"Nooo!" she protested. Shouting was all she could do as I had completely drained her of power. Genny shrank down and was sucked into the tube.

"Gotcha!" Kate said, slamming her hand down on the tube. Kate looked at me. "Good job, Tammy!"

I felt the raw power. I could see everything. I could see the very strings of energy that held the molecules of the world together. Time, space, and reality were all now mine to play with. They would jump and twist to my every thought and whim. Yeah, I liked this!

"Okay, Tammy great job!" Kate repeated. "Now just point to the tube and let me trap the power in there!"

"Come on, sis. Give it up. We won!" Barry said.

"Come on, Tammy," Rover said.

All the people outside started chanting, "Tammy! Tammy! Tammy!"

Turning to them, I ordered. "Bow down to me!" My voice was so malicious, so strong.

The mob of people all bowed at once. I liked it. No, I loved it. The world was mine to command now!

"Oh no, this is bad, so bad," Kate said.

I looked at the mob. Then I looked at Kate. My power felt SO good! Then, I laughed harder than I ever had in my entire life. O-M-G this felt amazing!

CHAPTER SEVENTEEN
BARRY

Oh boy, this was bad. Very bad.

My sister was now the bad guy, well, gal. It really wasn't her fault. She had taken on too much power. No human was meant to have that kind of power. I had to talk her down and bring her back to us. But that was going to be easier said than done. At the moment, Tammy was crackling and giddy with power.

Kate rushed over to her. "Great job Tammy. Now just let the power flow into the test tube and I will seal it for a LONG time."

Tammy shook her head. "No! I like this power!"

"But," Kate started to say. With a wave of her hand, Tammy turned her into a pig.

"Quiet. I'm keeping the power!"

I slowly approached my sister. "Sis, what are you doing? We have to seal the tube and trap Genny."

"No, we don't!' Tammy said glowing with power. "I control all of her power now! I am power!" she shouted. The earth rumbled.

Tammy snapped her fingers. Our house, which had been torn apart by Genny, snapped back to normal. She rubbed her hands together feverishly and asked me, "What should I do first, bro? World Peace? Or turn Maggie and her crew into piles of poo?"

"Those are two totally different courses of action," I told her.

Tammy shook her head. "Not really, they both make the world better!"

That was my in. My chance. I knew my sister well. She really did want to make the world a better place. She was a good person. Yeah, she felt anger towards the bullies in the world, but I guess I couldn't blame her.

"So, you don't like bullies," I said.

"Very good, bro. You really are smarter than you look or act."

"Thanks!"

"I don't think she meant it as a compliment," Rover said.

I grinned at him. "But that's how I'm going to take it. You see, we all get to choose how we react to other people. What we see in them. I

101

choose to see the good. I also focus on what I can control, and I don't worry about things I can't control." I said, looking at Tammy.

Tammy snapped her fingers. Instantly, we were standing on top of a mountain. "That's the thing brother, I control everything!" she told me.

"Do you?" I asked.

Another snap of her fingers and we stood in the middle of what seemed to be a Super Bowl game. All the players and people in the stands were frozen in place. Tammy pointed to the scoreboard. It showed the score: Tammy 100,000 World: 0.

Another snap of her fingers and we stood in the desert, but not just any desert. The Sahara. There were two groups of men and women firing at each other. Their bullets were also frozen in time. Tammy walked over and blew the bullets out of the air. She smiled at me.

"See Barry, I really do control everything."

She snapped her fingers. "You people love each other now."

The two sides dropped their weapons. They ran to each other and started hugging.

Tammy appeared next to me. She put her arm around me. "See brother, dear, it's all good. Problem solved."

"Is it really?" I asked.

Tammy pointed at the hugging troops. "Yes, they love each other now! I am totally awesome. I even took away my super B-O because I don't need it."

Shaking my head, I said, "You made them do that. You just changed them from troops into puppets. I'm not sure that's better."

She snapped her fingers again. We were back in my bedroom. A wave of her hand and my room smelled like fresh baked cookies. "See, I even made your room smell better!" Tammy told me.

I grinned. "True. I'll give you that. But you see sis, I kind of like the stink in my room. Yeah it stunk, but I liked the stink."

"Wait, what? How could you possibly like that?" Tammy asked with her eyes wide open.

"See Tammy, you have great power, but you don't have the wisdom or insight to use that power. You're just doing what you want willy nilly!"

"Nobody says willy nilly?" Tammy said.

I held up a finger. I took a chance here. A chance that my twin sister wouldn't turn me into a pile of poo. "You, Tammy, have become a bully. You are forcing your will on others, whether they like it or not."

"No! That can't be!" Tammy shouted. The force of her voice sent me flying across the room and smashing into the wall. Luckily, I still had my ninja skills which allowed me to take the fall without much damage. Still, I laid there letting Tammy think about what she had just done.

"NO!" Tammy shouted, running over to me. "Barry, are you okay?"

Lifting my head up, I told her, "I will be, once you realize you have become what you hate. A bully!"

A tear rolled down Tammy's cheek. "I don't want to be a bully! I don't want to hurt people, even other bullies! But I don't know how to get rid of this power now!" she cried.

Kate popped back into human form. Stretching, she said, "Finally! Now that's an experience I don't want to relive. Where's the test tube?"

Rover picked up the tube and brought it over to Kate. "I hope you don't mind that I sealed it. We don't want any genie leaking out."

"How did you do that?" Kate asked.

"I'm a dog who's always been good with his paws!" Rover said.

Kate took the test tube from Rover. She pointed it at Tammy. "Okay, Tammy, let the power flow out of you!" she said. "It will flow through the seal!"

"But I like it!" Tammy insisted.

I locked eyes with my sister. "No, you don't! It makes you what you hate."

"But I can control it. We can use this power to fight bullies. To make the world better." She shuddered.

I kept my eyes locked on her. "If that's true, then you could give up the power. We don't need super powers to defeat bullies. We just need to cooperate, use communication, and work together."

"Take a breath and exhale," Kate ordered.

Tammy took a deep breath. Then another. She pointed her finger towards the test tube. A glowing bright blue beam of energy appeared on her finger tip. The beam pulsated, then stretched out towards Kate. The energy from Tammy's finger flowed into the bottle, where it stopped.

There was a bright flash. My room's normal smell returned. Kate lifted the tube up to the light and smiled. "We did it! The power is contained!"

I went to the window. The people on the street were acting like normal, going to and fro. Yeah, I know Tammy would tell me that people didn't say to and fro, but I did. I smiled when I saw Mr. Powder out in his yard waving his arms at the people passing by.

I put my arm around Tammy. "How do you feel?"

"Frankly. I'm relieved," she said. "That was way too much power for me to handle. It took all my energy not to just make everybody go away and leave me alone. The only reason I didn't was because I was afraid I wouldn't be able to bring anybody back. I didn't want to be alone in the world."

I laughed. "Don't worry sis, you'll never be alone."

Kate walked over to us. "You two did great. Now we can keep Genny in her bottle for thousands of years. She won't be able to tempt anyone or take over the world for a long time."

I nodded. "Hopefully by then humanity will be able to handle her!" I said.

"Let's hope!" Kate said.

Tammy's and my phones both vibrated. We saw a text from Mom saying she would be home early.

"Looks like Mom never went on her trip," Tammy said.

"That's correct," Kate said. "Everything has gone back to how it was before you released Genny. It's how it was meant to be."

"Well, not everything," Rover said. "It appears I can still talk." With his nose, he pointed to a picture of a creepy eye on the wall. "Oh, and that's new."

Check out a preview of the next book in the

FRIGHTVISION

series:

Framed For Life

(Featuring the nightmares of
Artemis Hart & Bruce Zanders)

CHAPTER ONE

Josh was in the middle of watching his favorite gamer Let's Play Video. "Hurry up, Josh. I want you to take these cookies while they're still hot."

Ugh. Josh tried pretending that he couldn't hear his mom calling, but she was on to him.

"You've always told me not to talk to strangers. Sorry, Mom, I don't think it's safe," he said—half as a joke, half hoping she'd fall for the excuse.

"The Waters aren't strangers; they're your new neighbors. It's hard moving to a new place. We need to show them that they are welcome. Come on, Josh. Just go take them the basket and tell them that we're here if they need anything."

"Can't you do it? They'd rather talk to you anyway."

"No. I've got work I need to finish. And besides, I think it'll be good for you to go introduce yourself and meet new people. You're always so glued to your phone."

Josh grumbled that he met plenty of people online who actually liked the same stuff he did. His mom wasn't having it. It was time to admit defeat. Slowly, he got up and put on his shoes. They were too big and he felt like he was wearing clown shoes every time he put them on. His dad always bought him clothes that were at least one size too big, "to give him room to grow." Maybe he could spend the summer cutting grass for some of his neighbors. Then he'd be able to buy his own clothes for school next year.

He sighed and checked the mirror in the hallway. His blonde hair was a complete mess. He tried to push it down flat against his head, but it just made things worse and he gave up. At least he was wearing his go to t-shirt that featured his favorite video game character, who had messy blond hair just like Josh, and carried a shining sword and shield. Josh grabbed the basket of oatmeal cookies–*I thought mom wanted to make a* good *impression, blah!*—and headed next door.

It was good that someone had finally bought that old place. It was a nice house, with a small front porch that had white columns on either side. But it had been sitting empty for so long that the pale blue paint was starting to turn grey and peel, and the trees and bushes sat wildly overgrown. As he climbed the steps, he couldn't help but notice that the door was ajar. The neighbors must have left it open while they were unpacking. Just as he was reaching out to knock on it, the wind picked up, and the door swung open, as if inviting him in.

"Hello?" Josh called. No one answered.

He stuck his head in to see if anyone was around. The place was empty. All he could see were boxes stacked to the ceiling. Each one was labeled with its final destination. Living room. Kitchen. Bedroom. Only one box had been opened. It looked worn and older than the other boxes, and it was the only one without a label on it.

Surely with the door being left open, someone had to be here.

"Is anyone home?" Josh called out. Still, no response. Slowly, he started inching his way inside, craning to see if maybe someone was upstairs.

As he got closer though, he couldn't help but take a peek into the opened box. It seemed to be filled with odds and ends for house decorating. In it he could see a few little statues and figurines like he had seen displayed in his grandmother's glass cabinets. But they weren't nearly as cute as his grandmother's baby angel collection. These looked like something from a monster movie.

There was one figurine of a woman with three heads who was holding a snake like a baby. A big ugly cyclops with one eye was lying next to her. There was a centaur with the body of a horse and the head of a man. And, weirdest of all, a skull wearing a purple top hat.

Josh figured this family must be into some kind of role-playing games and decided to dig deeper to see what other kinds of cool games they might have. Maybe if they had the same game sets, they could all play together! Surely just a little peeking wouldn't hurt. Besides, no one was around anyway. He set the basket of cookies down and started rummaging. But instead of board games, he found some dried flowers and a couple of jars filled with spices and liquids. Josh made a face when he saw one was full of pickled pigs feet. Under all of that were plain black and white curtains or table cloths, Josh couldn't tell which. Lifting the fabric revealed a stack of books with strange writing on them. They looked old and smelled of leather. There didn't seem to be any more game stuff in here and he was just about to give up when something glistening in gold at the bottom caught his eye. Curious, he grabbed the item and pulled it out from the bottom of the box. Holding it up, he could see that it was a gold framed picture of a girl that looked to be about the same age as him. She was really pretty too with a little button nose, sparkling blue eyes, and a big bow in her curly blonde hair.

"Hello!"

"YUARGH!" He jumped, trying to hide the picture behind his back and knocked over the basket with his foot, spilling cookies everywhere. Instinctively, he jammed the frame into his cargo pocket.

A girl appeared in front of him. He must not have seen her between all of the boxes that were piled up. Once his heart stopped pounding from the shock, he realized that it was the same exact girl from the picture. And she was even prettier in person.

Way to go, Mr. Smooth, he thought to himself. Here he is, lucky enough to have this girl moving in right next door, and the first time they meet she catches him breaking into their house and going through their stuff.

To make matters worse, he had just screamed and almost wet his pants in front of her. It almost made him mad how cute she was with her nose wrinkling and her curly hair bouncing as she giggled at him.

Josh could feel his face turning a bright shade of red. "My parents wanted me to bring those over," he mumbled, desperate to get out of there.

"Don't worry about the mess, my mom will clean it up," she reassured him. "My name is Beatrice," she said, thankfully changing the subject.

"I'm Josh," he replied.

"Hi Josh," she smiled. She looked as though she was just about to say something else, but instead exclaimed, "Ah! I love that game!"

"Huh?" Josh was confused at first. But then he followed her gaze. "Oh, my shirt! Yeah, this is from the original game. I absolutely love it!" he said grinning from ear to ear.

"What level did you get to?" She asked, bouncing with excitement.

"Level 12," he said with a smirk, glad that he could brag about his high score. There was no way this girl could beat that!

"Ah-ha! I've gotten to level 14!"

"No way!"

"Yup!"

"Well I guess you'll just have to prove it to me sometime," he said, crossing his arms.

"Oh, you are so on!" she said, taunting him and giggling. Suddenly her smile dropped. "But I don't know when. I can't seem to find any of my stuff lately," she said with a sigh.

"It's so frustrating. I don't know what my parents have done with everything."

"Maybe they sold it all so they could afford to buy a bigger house." Josh joked, trying to impress her with his amazing humor. She just stared at him, while he stood frozen with a dumb smirk on his face.

"At this point I wouldn't be surprised. I can't find any of my stuff. Here, I'll show you what I mean. The upstairs is completely empty."

Did she really want to take him upstairs? Josh wasn't sure what to do. He knew he was just getting a tour of the house, but it felt weird to go upstairs with a girl that he hardly knew when no one else was home.

Unsure what to do, he slowly followed her up the stairs, and she led him into an empty room with a big window that was set off in a little cubby that could be perfect for a cozy window seat. "See, this is supposed to be my room and none of my stuff is here. I don't even have a bed!" she frowned.

"Don't worry, I'm sure your parents will get your room all set up in no time. They just have to go through all the boxes first."

"All of those ugly boxes. I don't know what my parents are planning to do with everything, but I really don't like how they've packed everything up."

Josh wasn't sure what to say. He could imagine how hard it must be to have to pick up your whole life and move to a new place where you didn't know anyone. And he would be frustrated too, if his parents packed his stuff and he couldn't find any of it. At the same time, he knew that her parents would be getting everything in place as fast as they could. After all, they'd just moved in, and unpacking would take a little while.

He gave her a sympathetic look, "How about we go downstairs and I'll help you look through the boxes for your stuff?"

Beatrice smiled, "That would be great!"

They made their way back down the stairs, but just as they got to the bottom, he heard people walking up to the front door.

"My parents will be upset if they know that we've been here alone together! Go!" Beatrice whispered to him.

"Okay, I'll be back tomorrow!" he promised her. Then he quickly ran out the back door, just barely missing her parents.

As he sneaked around the corner of the house, he peaked in and saw them from the window. Her parents seemed furious about the mess from the cookies and all the things he'd taken out of the box. He could see Beatrice trying to explain, but they looked like they were just ignoring her. He should have just cleaned up the mess instead of leaving it there. What had he been thinking?

He continued to watch as Mrs. Waters went over to the open box and began flailing her arms and pointing. Josh looked down at his bulging cargo pocket. The picture! It was still in his pocket. He had forgotten to put it back. Mrs. Waters must have noticed it was missing, and she was really upset. He felt bad, but it was too late to put it back. And besides, now he had a picture of Beatrice. Shrugging and smiling, he decided to keep it.

43966565R00076

Made in the USA
Middletown, DE
01 May 2019